✦PRINCESS

Beauties in Bloom

By Melissa Lagonegro
Illustrated by Peter Emslie

A Random House PICTUREBACK® Book
Random House New York

Published in the United States by Random House Children's Books, a division of Random House, Inc., New York, and simultaneously in Canada by Random House of Canada Limited, Toronto, in conjunction with Disney Enterprises, Inc.
PICTUREBACK, RANDOM HOUSE, and the Random House colophon are registered trademarks of Random House, Inc.
Library of Congress Control Number: 2002102374 ISBN: 0-7364-2094-0
www.randomhouse.com/kids/disney Printed in the United States of America 18 17 16 15 14 13 12 11

Walt Disney's
Snow White
and the Seven Dwarfs

"What a lovely spring morning!" exclaimed Snow White with a smile.

The sun was shining, the birds were singing, and the sweet smell of flowers filled the air.

"It's a perfect day for a walk in the woods," Snow White told her forest friends.

Together, they headed off to enjoy the many sights and scents of spring.

Before long, Snow White and her friends came upon a field of tulips swaying in the breeze.

"Oh, I *must* pick just a few," the young princess said as she stopped to admire the flowers.

When her basket was filled with flowers, Snow White continued into the woods. Suddenly, she heard a sound. *Quack! Quack! Quack!*

"Why, it's a mother duck and her little ducklings," said Snow White.

Snow White giggled as she watched the baby ducks drink and splash in a flowing stream.

"The Dwarfs will certainly be thirsty when they return home from work," she said. "Perhaps I should bring them some cool water."

When her pitcher was full, Snow White stood up. She spotted a perfect gooseberry bush across the stream.

"These berries look so ripe and sweet!" said the pleased princess as she began to pick them.

"Oh, dear. My basket is filled to the brim!" said Snow White. "It's time to head back to the cottage."

As she walked home, Snow White smiled. "What's the perfect way to end this perfect spring day?" she wondered.

When the Dwarfs came home from work that afternoon, they found a wonderful surprise—a picnic! Snow White and her friends shared stories about their day over a freshly baked gooseberry pie. It *was* the perfect end to a lovely spring day!

Walt Disney's
Cinderella

Spring had arrived, and it was time for Cinderella to take care of the family garden. Pulling weeds and planting seeds wasn't much fun, but Cinderella always enjoyed being outside near the sweet-smelling flowers and budding plants.

While Cinderella worked, her stepsisters were busy preparing for the Prince's Royal Garden Party.

"I look so pretty in my new spring bonnet," declared Drizella.

"I will win the Prince's heart when he sees me in mine," cried Anastasia.

Cinderella watched as her stepsisters climbed into their carriage.

"I wish I could go to the Royal Garden Party, too," she told Gus and Jaq sadly. "But I have too much work to do."

Gus and Jaq wanted to do something to make Cinderella feel better. With the help of the other animals, they made her a special surprise out of an old straw hat.

"My very own spring bonnet!" Cinderella cheered. "Oh, it's just beautiful!"

After finishing all her chores, Cinderella spent the rest of the day enjoying the wonders of the garden.

"Look how the bumblebees buzz from flower to flower," she said to the mice.

Cinderella spotted a baby robin on the grass.

"Poor little thing, I'll help you get home," she said lovingly.

Cinderella gently placed the baby bird back in its nest.

Suddenly, clouds filled the sky and rain began to fall. It was a spring shower!

Cinderella, Gus, and Jaq danced in the warm rain and splashed in the puddles. They watched the beads of water roll off flower petals and decorate a beautiful spiderweb. It was such fun!

When the rain stopped, Cinderella heard her stepsisters returning from the party. They were sopping wet and covered in mud!

"That was the worst party ever!" exclaimed Drizella.

"The Prince didn't even notice me!" cried Anastasia. "And worst of all, my bonnet is ruined!"

As the clouds passed and the sun came back out, a beautiful rainbow filled the sky.

"I guess my wish came true," Cinderella told Gus and Jaq with a smile. "This truly was the best garden party ever!"